Horse Power

Horse Power

Ann Walsh

Orca currents

ORCA BOOK PUBLISHERS

Library and Archives Canada Cataloguing in Publication

Walsh, Ann, 1942-
Horse power / written by Ann Walsh.
(Orca currents)

ISBN 978-1-55143-883-2 (bound).--ISBN 978-1-55143-881-8 (pbk.)

I. Title. II. Series.
PS8595.A585H67 2007 jC813'.54 C2007-903833-6

First published in the United States, 2007
Library of Congress Control Number: 2007930412

Summary: Wild horses couldn't drag Callie to this protest, but her mom can.

Mixed Sources
Cert no. SW-COC-001271
© 1996 FSC

Orca Book Publishers is dedicated to preserving the environment and has printed this book on paper certified by the Forest Stewardship Council.

Orca Book Publishers gratefully acknowledges the support for its publishing programs provided by the following agencies: the Government of Canada through the Canada Book Fund and the Canada Council for the Arts, and the Province of British Columbia through the BC Arts Council and the Book Publishing Tax Credit.

Cover design by Teresa Bubela
Cover photography by Masterfile

ORCA BOOK PUBLISHERS
PO Box 5626, Stn. B
Victoria, BC Canada
V8R 6S4

ORCA BOOK PUBLISHERS
PO Box 468
Custer, WA USA
98240-0468

www.orcabook.com
Printed and bound in Canada.

13 12 11 10 • 5 4 3 2

Chapter One

"Where's Mom? Why isn't she here?"

"Hi, Callie. Your mom's busy," said my Uncle Ken.

Something was wrong. My mother *always* meets me at the airport when I get home from Dad's place in Ottawa.

"*Busy*? Too busy to meet her only daughter who has been away for a whole month? Peter, what's going on?" I asked, using his real name and adding "please" for good measure. He isn't really my uncle and his name isn't really Ken, but it could have been. His mother wanted to call him Ken, but his father objected. Ken Dawl. I guess if he'd been a girl she would have wanted to name him Barbie. Some people's mothers!

"Isn't that your bag?" Uncle Ken/Peter Dawl lunged for a blue suitcase. He grabbed it, pulled out the handle and began to wheel it behind him. "Come on."

He pushed past the other passengers crowding the baggage claim area and trotted on ahead of me. I caught up with him outside and followed him toward the parking lot.

"Slow down!" I called. "Aren't we getting a cab?" Mom doesn't own a car, so we take a taxi from the airport. Peter doesn't own a car either.

"We don't need a cab today, Callie," he said.

"Did you buy that sports car you were talking about?" I asked. "Did you? How did you get the money?" Peter was a reporter for a small community newspaper, *The Westside Tribune*. I knew he didn't make a lot of money, but maybe he got a raise.

In the parking area, he stopped and rummaged in his pocket. "Where'd I put the keys?" He pulled out a key ring, dropped it, picked it up and started to open the door of…

"You're kidding!" I said. "Please tell me we aren't going to ride in *that*. You didn't buy…"

"A van," he said proudly.

The van was so old it looked as if it had been used to deliver ice back in the days before refrigerators. It had rust spots around the wheels, and one side looked as if it had banged into something over and over. The van was old, rusty and dented, but the worst part was that it was purple. Really, really bright purple.

"You're kidding," I said again. "You've *got* to be joking."

My "uncle" looked hurt. "It's a free ride home, Callie," he said. "And this baby's in good mechanical shape. She purrs along."

He pulled on the sliding door. It opened slowly, making metal-on-metal screeching noises as it moved.

"Purr? That's a purr?"

He ignored me. "You have to get in the back, then climb over to the front. The front door doesn't open on your side."

I was seriously considering taking the bus home. But I'd spent the last of the money Dad had given me on junk food.

I got into the back of the purple van, climbed into the front seat and rummaged in my backpack for the wraparound sunglasses I'd bought at the beginning of the summer I thought

I would look cool when I got a ride on our neighbor's motorbike. But Mr. Wilson hadn't offered me a ride, not even once. However, the sunglasses were a good disguise.

"Are you sure this thing runs?" I asked.

"Of course," he said indignantly. "It's old—it was my mother's—but it's in good shape. Except for where Mom used to bang into a post beside her parking spot— that's why the door doesn't open. I've kept it in storage until now, but your mother..."

Which brought me back to my question. "Okay, explain. Why is Mom so busy she can't come and meet me? Is she okay?"

"She's fine," said Peter as he started the van. "Just busy, packing. She's leaving this afternoon."

"Oh, great," I said. "If she'd told me she was going away, I'd have stayed at Dad's."

"But you're going with your mom."

"No! I just got home. I don't want to go anywhere."

"Tell that to your mother," Peter said. "Or try to. Good luck."

He had a point. When Mom wanted to do something—or wanted me to do something—it got done. There was no arguing with her.

I sighed. I hadn't been back home for twenty minutes and already I was sighing. "Where are we going? And why?"

"I'm not exactly sure about the where, except I know it's in the country. I'm coming too. Actually, I'm driving you."

"Driving? This purple thing? Don't you have a job or something else to do?" I asked hopefully.

"I'm on holiday. This trip could be fun, and I know there's a good story in it. There's always a good story when your mother takes on a project."

"Project?" I didn't like the sound of that. "What kind of project?"

Peter grinned at me. "Another protest, Callie."

"Oh, no!" I couldn't believe it. The last protest Mom organized was to save a tree growing on our neighbor's property. Reporters, TV crews and even the police had shown up.

The reporters had used my real name in the newspapers and on TV. My friends were still teasing me about it. "So, Calendula, what's your mother up to these days? Have the police been to your house lately, *Calendula*?"

"Wasn't saving that tree enough for Mom?"

Peter shook his head. "Apparently not. She's moving on to bigger things. This time she wants to save a school."

Chapter Two

I kept my head down all the way home.
I don't think anyone recognized me.

Mom was on the front porch,
surrounded by boxes, suitcases and
plastic bags.

"Hey, Callie, it's good to have you
home. Hope your clothes are clean—
you *did* do laundry at your father's,
didn't you? Peter, we need to pick up

camping foamies. I can't find the ones Callie and I used when we went camping in the Rockies."

"We're going *camping*?" I asked.

"Not exactly. Although we will be sleeping in the tent on the school grounds."

She stepped around piles of stuff and came down the stairs. "I missed you," she said, hugging me.

I didn't hug her back. "I hate camping. You know that."

"This is different, Callie. This will be a protest."

"I don't want to protest. And I don't want to sleep in the tent with you. You snore."

Mom stopped hugging me. "I do not!" she said.

She does snore and she knows it. She also knows I hate sleeping in a tent on the lumpy ground and having to stumble in the dark to a stinky outhouse in the middle of the night. I don't even like campfires. The smoke makes me sneeze.

"I could stay with Grandma," I said.

She looked hurt. "This is a family trip, Callie. Besides, you know your grandmother's building has a rule about kids being there for more than a night. They *do* allow pets to live there though. I've never thought about it before now, but that's unfair. Maybe it's a human rights violation. Or animal rights. We should organize a letter-writing campaign and…"

"Okay, how about I hide out at Grandma's and start writing letters about the discrimination against kids?"

"Your grandmother is going on a trip herself. You can't stay with her."

"Then I'll stay with Josie," I said. Josie is my best friend. "She won't mind."

"She's away with her parents."

I had forgotten that. "I'll...I'll stay here by myself. I can do it, Mom. I'll take the garbage out on Tuesdays, and I won't stay up late. Too late, anyway."

Mom glared at me. "No deal. You're coming with me, so stop arguing."

"I won't go! You can't make me."

Mom got that "or else" look on her face. "Want to bet? Any more arguments from you and you'll be grounded for a month as soon as we get back."

I didn't say anything. I hate it when Mom pulls that "I'm in charge of you" attitude. I also hate being grounded.

"I'm glad that's settled," said Mom. "Aunt Gerry will be glad to see you."

"We're going to *Aunt Gerry's*? No one told me that."

Aunt Gerry is my Aunt Geranium. All the women in my family, for generations back, are named after flowers. There's Grandma Rose and my mother, Dian (Dianthus). And me,

Callie (Calendula). Aunt Gerry is tall and muscular and loves horses. She didn't go to art school like Mom. She left home as soon as she finished high school and got a job on a ranch. Then she married the rancher, my Uncle Mike. Eventually they had my cousin, Del. Even though Mom is younger than Aunt Gerry, I'm older than Del.

I'm only a few months older, but Del's a grade below me in school. She's starting grade seven in September, but I'm going into high school.

We don't look much alike—Del's tall like her mom and doesn't have red hair. I'm the only one in my family with red hair. Del and I don't like the same music or TV shows and Del wants to go riding all the time. Riding a horse, not a motorbike or an ATV or something cool. Del doesn't even own a bicycle. I never liked her much, and after what happened last summer, I *really* don't like her.

"Could we go camping somewhere else?" I asked. "Anywhere else?"

"No, Gerry and Del need our help."

"Why?"

"Del's school is being closed."

"Really? Sounds good to me."

"Callie, that isn't funny." Mom glared at me. I wondered if she was going to give me her "Education is your most valuable resource" lecture, but she went back to organizing Peter.

"That big box is groceries. Bedding is in the plastic bags, and the cooler is in the kitchen. It's nearly packed." The two of them scurried up and down the steps, stuffing boxes and bags into Peter's van.

"Hurry up, Callie," Mom called. "Take those new clothes out of your suitcase—don't glare at me like that. I know you conned your father into buying you new clothes again. Make sure you have two pairs of jeans, your old ones, and pack a warm jacket.

The nights will be cold. Oh, and see if you can find the mosquito repellent."

"Mosquitoes? Scorpions? Rattle-snakes? Maybe even rabid grizzly bears? I can hardly wait."

"Drop the sarcasm, Callie. Gerry says the bugs aren't bad this summer. Now go pack. It's a long drive and we need to get started."

I sighed again. Like it or not, I was going camping. Cold nights, snoring mothers, bloodthirsty mosquitoes, stinky outhouses and all. Not to mention having to listen to my cousin go on and on about her horse. Or her 4-H projects.

But there was nothing I could do. I had to go. Sighing again, I picked up my suitcase and went in the house.

Chapter Three

Mom was right about one thing. It *was* a long drive. I sat in the back of the van wearing my sunglasses, my head down, plugged into my music. After a while, I decided that there wasn't much chance of my friends seeing me, so I took off the sunglasses and looked at the scenery. The highway curled along a river and through a twisting canyon.

Then it straightened out, and the scenery got boring, nothing but trees to look at. Then I fell asleep.

When I woke up, the sky was pink and gold in the sunset. I yawned, stretched and asked, "Are we there yet?"

"Look for yourself," snapped Mom. She hated that question.

We were bumping up the gravel driveway to Del's school. It was small, only four classrooms and a tiny gym. A few trees and dusty bushes dotted the hillside around it, but that's all there was. Just the school, playground, parking lot and a driveway rolling down to the highway. If students forgot their lunches there was no running to the corner store—there *was* no corner store.

"Dian! You made it." Aunt Gerry's voice was loud. It always is. "Where'd you get the van? Who's that driving? Isn't he a bit young for you?"

My aunt wrenched open the van's sliding door. Mom climbed over the front seat, pushed past me and got out. "Gerry, that's Peter, I told you about him. He's a *friend*, a reporter. It's his van."

"Friend, huh?" said my aunt under her breath. Then she stuck her head inside the van. "Hi, Callie, come on out. I bet you've grown. Hello, Peter. I'm Gerry. Thanks for coming. We need media exposure."

"He's just a newspaper reporter," I said. "You should get TV reporters if you want publicity."

"Don't say *just*, Callie," Peter said.

"Welcome to Shady Glen, Peter. My, you are young, aren't you? First job?"

"Actually—," Peter began.

Aunt Gerry didn't let him finish. She shook his hand so hard I saw him wince. "Good to meet you, Peter."

She pulled me out of the van and gave me a big hug. "Run along and find Del, Callie. She's over there." My aunt gestured to a group of people gathered around a campfire. I spotted my cousin, Del—short for Delphinium. She was so tall you couldn't miss her.

Del didn't come over to say hello. Good. Sometimes she smelled like one of her 4-H projects. Or more like hay when it comes out the other end of an animal. Getting too close to Del could ruin your appetite for days.

"Go see your cousin," said my mom. "You have a lot of catching up to do."

I wasn't planning to "catch up" with my cousin or even speak to her. I was still mad at her. I bent over and pretended to tie my shoelaces. Maybe if I stalled long enough I'd find a way to escape.

There were tents set up on the lawn in front of the school and three trailers in the parking lot. The campfire was behind the school near the swings.

Kids' faces moved in and out of the firelight as they swung back and forth. Del sat on a chunk of wood, back from the campfire. Behind her, tied to a tree, was Radish. I hated that horse. He was evil.

I retied my shoes twice and then straightened up. Del was staring at me. So was Radish. Did he remember me? Horses couldn't remember things that happened a year ago, could they?

Radish made a snickering noise. It sounded like a laugh. Last summer I had ridden him. I hadn't wanted to ride anything except Uncle Mike's four-wheeler, but Mom nagged me about how it was a shame to be in the heart of horse country and not at least *try* horseback riding. After all, she told me over and over again, doing something new would make me a more rounded person and enrich my life.

Mom was right. Sort of. My head

was "rounded" by a bump so big that I had to go to the hospital. My wardrobe was "enriched" too. I had to buy new jeans because my old ones were ruined. Radish tossed me off his back as soon as I got in the saddle. I bumped my head on a fence post and rolled down a hill. My life was definitely *not* enriched when my cousin and her horse laughed at me while I lay in the dirt trying not to cry. I could have been dead, and they laughed. Don't tell me horses can't laugh. They can. They do.

I was still trying to avoid talking to Del, when Mom called me to help set up the tent.

"Be right there, Mom," I yelled cheerfully. "Glad to help." Mom gasped in surprise, and Aunt Gerry looked puzzled.

But I'd do anything, even be really helpful, to avoid talking to Del.

Chapter Four

By the time we got the tent up my relatives had gone home. So far so good, I thought. Maybe I could do this whole trip without speaking to Del. I'd work on it.

Even though I'd napped in the van, I was tired. We made a trip to the outhouse and then settled down to sleep.

Or try to sleep. Mom snored. I kept kicking her, trying to make her stop. When she was quiet, I heard noises outside. A howling, far away. Then hooting sounds, much closer. In one of the tents, a baby cried, and a man in another tent snored even louder than Mom. A mosquito buzzed around my head, ignoring the repellent I'd sprayed all over myself. Mom snored.

She woke up early. After she left the tent, I rolled over and tried to catch up on the sleep I'd missed during the night. But Mom wasn't gone long.

"Callie, get up. There's work to do."

"Work?" I was barely awake, and I didn't like the sound of that word. "Work?"

"Hurry up, we're on breakfast this morning."

"How can we be *on* anything? We just got here."

"I volunteered us," she answered cheerfully. "Here, I've brought you warm water. Wash up. Then come and help me at the barbecue. You can flip the pancakes."

"Huh?" Mom wasn't making any sense. You don't barbecue pancakes.

"I'll be in the big tent around the side of the school. Hurry up. I need help and I can't find Peter."

I found my clothes beside my sleeping bag and got dressed. Then I splashed water on my face and pulled my fingers through my hair. It was too much trouble to look for my comb.

Mom actually *was* barbecuing pancakes. At least she was pouring batter onto a huge griddle on top of a barbecue. She had also found Peter. He was standing in front of another barbecue, grumpily poking sausages with a fork. Poking them as if they were going to leap off the barbecue and run away. He had slept in the van, and he looked as if he'd had as rotten a night as I had.

"Callie, wash your hands in that bucket and then come and help me."

"I already washed."

"Do it again. You're going to be working with food." I dipped my hands into the bleach-smelling water. Then I took the flipper Mom thrust at me.

"When the bubbles pop on the pancakes, they're ready to be flipped," she instructed. "Call me when you need more batter poured."

She breezed off to tell Peter how to poke the sausages. I stood as far away from the hot barbecue as I could, watching bubbles form on the pancakes.

The cook tent began to fill up. People helped themselves to food and took their plates outside to the picnic tables.

I watched more bubbles and flipped more pancakes. And got hungry.

"Morning, Callie. Get yourself some food. I'll take over here." I jumped when I heard Aunt Gerry's loud voice behind me.

"Thanks," I said, handing her the flipper.

"Dian still snore like a freight train passing through a tunnel?" my aunt asked. "Boy, I remember her shaking the whole house at night. Even the cat wouldn't sleep in her room."

"She still snores," I admitted.

"Would you like to come to our house and sleep in the top bunk in Del's room?"

"Um…"

"You don't have to ride a horse, Callie. It's just a chance to sleep in a real bed. Or you can stay with your mother and have another sleepless night.

Your choice." Aunt Gerry began tossing pancakes in the air like a chef on the Food Channel.

"Um," I said again, wondering if I should try to explain. But what would I say? That I didn't like my cousin? That I hated her horse? That I was never going to speak to Del again, never mind having a sleepover with her?

Aunt Gerry turned and stared at me. She frowned. "I understand," she said. "You're still ticked off about falling off Radish."

"I didn't *fall*. He threw me. On purpose," I said indignantly. "And Del didn't have to laugh like that."

"Okay, I get it. Your dignity was hurt."

"My dignity's fine. My head was hurt, remember?" I started to walk away, but my aunt called me back.

"I'm sorry, Callie," she said. "I know it wasn't a good experience for you."

"Oh, but I *love* shopping for new jeans," I said. "I just don't love what I had to go through to get that particular pair." I reached up and rubbed my head, reminding her of how I'd suffered.

My aunt sighed loudly. I stared at her, amazed. "I do that too."

"Sigh? So does Del," she said. "We Powers women are great sighers."

My aunt took a deep breath and let it out noisily. "Yup, I can do it pretty loudly. Let's hear your best effort."

I let out a huge sigh.

"Not bad." She grinned. "But your mother never sighs. Somehow she missed out on the family sighing gene."

"As long as I didn't get Mom's snoring gene, I don't care if she sighs or not," I said.

"What's that burning smell? Oh, shoot!" said my aunt, turning back to pancakes that were smoking and turning black. "We need more batter over here, Dian," she called. "This batch got a bit crispy."

She scooped the burnt pancakes off the grill and Mom poured more batter. "We're almost out of pancake mix, Gerry. Keep an eye on these."

After Mom bustled away, my aunt sighed again. "Look, Callie, I know you and Del are very different." This time she didn't look at me as she spoke. "Your mother and I are different too. Dian likes pottery and painting and all that artsy stuff—she always did. I like the smell of dew on the morning grass and riding fast so I can feel the wind in my hair. I wanted a horse of my own from the time I was ten. All your mother wanted was pierced ears and her own potting wheel."

"She still has both," I said.

"I know. And I still want horses around me. But in spite of all our differences, Dian and I became friends as well as sisters. Maybe you and Del will also grow into a friendship."

"You want me to take over flipping the pancakes again?" I asked.

"Changing the subject? I see. Okay, decide later about spending the night with us. But I'll finish the pancakes. You grab something to eat. Today is going to be a busy, busy day. Get some fodder in you."

"Thanks," I said and went for breakfast. The pancakes were excellent. I ate six and was thinking about going back for more when I heard a low rumbling sound. Like thunder, only the sun was shining and the sky was clear.

"What's that?" I asked.

No one answered, so I went to find out for myself.

The noise grew louder. I held my hands over my ears as six large motorbikes wheeled into the parking lot.

On the back of one of the bikes perched a passenger, wearing a metallic red helmet with a tinted face piece. The driver climbed off the bike and then held out his hand to help his passenger dismount. They both stretched and removed their helmets. As the red helmet came off, I couldn't believe what I was seeing.

"Grandma? *Grandma!*"

Chapter Five

"Callie, it's good to see you. Come and meet my friends."

The other kids stared at me. Del tried to hide behind a camper. "Del's here too," I said. "Don't forget about her."

"Really? Oh, there you are, Del. Give me a hug. It's so good to see my granddaughters together. Who's tallest? Why, Callie, I think you are. But Del is certainly the…um, what *is* that smell? Is there something on your shoe, Del?"

Del glared at me as Grandma squeezed her in a bear hug.

I smiled and stayed out of Grandma's reach.

"Callie, you remember Leon, don't you?" The driver of the motorbike was tall and wore his long gray hair in a ponytail. He took a pair of wraparound sunglasses from his pocket, put them on and nodded at me.

"I remember you, Callie," he said.

He was one of the bikers who had come to Mom's tree protest. "Leon, this is my other granddaughter, Del," said my grandma.

"What are you doing here, Gran?" asked Del, backing away from her. "We didn't know you were coming."

"Leon was up for a ride," she answered. "When I told him what was happening to your school, he thought it would be a cool idea to help save it. The way he helped with the fuss about the tree."

"But the bikers were on the *other* side of that protest, Gran!" I said. "They wanted to cut the tree down."

"Well, it doesn't matter now, does it? That business is over. Anyway, yesterday Leon and I rounded up some others from his biking club and here we are."

What? Did she say "Leon and I"? Did that mean they were going out together? Like, *dating?* It couldn't be like that.

But from the way they were smiling at each other it was like that.

"I don't get it," said another biker. "How can they close a school? Ain't it against the law?" This biker had a big stomach that hung out over his jeans. I recognized him too. He had also been there for the "tree business."

"Hi, Duke," I said.

"It's the Little Lady," he said. "Good to see ya."

"Welcome. Glad you brought your friends, Mother." Aunt Gerry shook hands with Duke, Leon and the other bikers. "You're just in time for the meeting."

"Meeting?" I asked.

"Our war council," said my aunt. "Every morning we go over new developments and review what's happened. More and more people are supporting the protest. It's only been two days, and look how many have joined us. We need to make sure the newcomers know all the facts. Hopefully the media will be here this afternoon."

"The media is already here," said Peter sulking. He smelled of sausages and his face was greasy.

"Facts?" said Duke. "Hey, I don't gotta learn stuff, do I, just because this is a school?"

"Don't worry, Duke. There's no exam," said my aunt. "Come on, everyone, it's nearly ten. Grab some coffee. There's food too, if anyone hasn't had breakfast. You older kids, take the little ones to the playground for a while."

I was about to say I hadn't come all this way and spent a sleepless night listening to Mom imitating a freight train just to babysit for free when Aunt Gerry said, "Not you, Callie. You need to know what's happening. You stay."

The other kids, including Del, went off to the playground. The bikers loaded up their plates—it was a good thing everyone else had already eaten. Camp chairs appeared, but there weren't enough, so some of us sat on the ground.

Duke joined me, balancing a full plate on his knees. "How you doing, kid?" he asked.

"I was doing fine until Mom dragged me up here."

"Tough," he said sympathetically.

"Listen up, everyone," said my aunt. "First, a hearty welcome to our new supporters." Everyone clapped. The bikers waved. Mom stood up and waved. Grandma stood up and blew kisses to everyone. I *didn't* stand up. I pretended I didn't know any of them.

The clapping stopped and my aunt said, "Okay, now let's review what's happened. I somehow got to be spokesperson…"

"That's probably because everyone can hear you, dear," said my grandma. "Although I don't know how many times I've told you that it isn't ladylike to shout like that."

"I'm not shouting," yelled my aunt, and everyone laughed.

She waited until we were quiet again. "Thank you all for being here. I counted heads, and this morning there are twenty-four adults and eight children, more or less."

There was clapping and cheering and one woman said, "I just heard the news last night, or I would have come sooner."

"I went to this school," said my Uncle Mike. "Now my daughter does. This place is a historic landmark."

"Yeah, and you're ancient history too, Mike," someone called, and there was more laughter.

"I don't understand," I said. "How can they close a school? And who are 'they' anyway?"

"Yeah!" said Duke. "Who is this 'they'?"

"Okay, here are the facts," said my aunt. "The school board (that's the 'they') has decided to close Shady Glen School."

"Why?" asked Duke. "Don't the kids who live around here have to go to school?"

"Yes, they do. But this is a very small school. Only four classrooms and half a principal—that means she's only a principal half of the time, Duke," she explained, before he could ask. "The rest of the time she teaches the grade six/seven class."

Duke nodded as if he had known that all along.

"All the classes have two grades. There aren't enough kids to make a full class of any one grade," my aunt explained. "Classes are small and getting smaller. Enrollment is dropping."

"Why does that mean that the school has to be closed?" asked Peter, busy scribbling in his notebook. "Aren't small classes the best learning environment? I thought small classes were a good thing."

"Small class sizes *are* good for learning," explained my aunt. "But small schools, especially the older small schools, are expensive to operate."

Duke and I said, "Huh?" together.

"In a larger community there are more students so the classes are bigger," someone explained. "Which means the school board gets more value for each teacher's salary."

"Fill 'em up," said Duke. There was silence. "I mean the classes," he explained. "They like to fill 'em up with kids, right?"

"Right," said my aunt. "Also, Shady Glen School needs a lot of expensive repairs."

"It doesn't look too bad," said Grandma's friend, Leon.

"It's what you can't see that costs money," said my aunt. "Like the septic system—that's how we get rid of waste water in the country, in case you city folks don't know. The septic system needs to be replaced, and the school needs a new roof."

"And the wiring needs to be redone so the kids can use computers in the classrooms," said someone else. "That's another big expense."

"Okay, so it costs a lot to keep this joint open," said Duke. "Yeah, and with only a few kids, that's a lotta bucks the school board has to spend on each kid."

"Exactly right, Duke," said Aunt Gerry. She sounded surprised. "A few years ago they built a new school in town. That school was built larger than was needed, because everyone thought the town would grow. Well, the town's grown all right, but most of the folks who moved here are retired. They don't have kids. Last year that fancy new school had four empty classrooms."

"I get it!" I said. "They—the school board—will save lots of money if they close Shady Glen School and make all the kids from here go to the new school.

They can move the kids into those empty classrooms!"

"Right," said my aunt again. "The teachers would transfer too, so they wouldn't lose their jobs."

"The town is about an hour's drive away?" asked Peter.

"Yes," said my aunt. "All of the students, even the little ones, will have to take the school bus. The trip will take more than an hour each way."

Peter whistled under his breath. "Wow. Add that to five hours of school and it's a long day for a little kid."

"It is," said my aunt. "There's no high school in Shady Glen, so our kids have to go to town to finish their schooling. But they're older then and can handle the long bus trip. It isn't fair to make a six-year-old spend three hours on a bus every single day."

"But Del already takes a bus," said my grandmother, sounding confused.

"About half of our students arrive by school bus, but they only travel a short distance," explained my aunt.

"The long bus trip means that during the winter the kids have to leave for school while it's still dark," said my uncle.

"And it will be dark again by the time they get home. Our winter days are very short," added my aunt.

There was a muttering of agreement. Duke looked so sad I thought he might cry.

"It ain't fair," he said. "It ain't fair at all."

Aunt Gerry nodded. "It also isn't fair that we didn't learn about this until a week ago when it was reported in the newspaper."

"The paper didn't have all the facts," said a new voice. Everyone turned around. We hadn't heard the newcomer's car because she hadn't driven a car. She arrived on a horse.

Pulling off her cowboy hat and running her fingers through her short gray hair, she went on, "Pardon me for butting in, but I guess you folks don't know the real reason your school board decided to close this school."

"What do you mean?" my aunt asked.

"Someone offered a lot of money to buy it. A real lot of money," said the woman.

"The school's going to be sold?" Aunt Gerry shook her head, bewildered. "But we thought…"

"I guess the school board tried to keep it a secret. Some fool millionaire wants to buy this school. Offered to pay twice what it was worth."

"But if they sell the school," said my grandmother, "then it can never be reopened, not even if…"

"Nope. Once it's sold, it's gone. The school board won't have to do any more arguing with you folks."

The woman put her hat back on and grinned. "Heck, it isn't often a stranger knows more gossip than the locals. Have a good day."

She nudged the horse. It turned around and, in a cloud of dust, they were gone.

"Who *was* that masked woman?" asked my grandmother.

"But she wasn't wearing a mask, was she?" I asked.

Chapter Six

After the woman rode away, everyone began talking at once, even though my aunt was yelling, "Order! Hey folks, one at a time. Order, please!"

I listened to the conversations going on around me and began to realize why people were so upset. Shady Glen School was more than just a place for kids to learn to read and do arithmetic.

The Girl Guides and the 4-H Club used the gym. The Duplicate Bridge and the Whirling Seniors met here. On Wednesday evenings, a group of writers used one of the classrooms, while the Woman's Auxiliary (whatever that was) met in another room. This school was a busy place, even on the weekends, when there were garage sales, yoga and Tai Chi classes.

If the school were sold, then it couldn't be used for any of these activities. Not only would the students have the long bus ride to the school in town, the adults would have to find another place for their clubs and hobbies.

Peter scribbled notes as he listened, shaking his head. "So this is a community loss," he said.

"That's what we've been trying to explain," said Aunt Gerry. "This school is the center of much of our lives."

She announced that she was going home to make some phone calls. My uncle went with her, muttering about the chores not doing themselves. He made Del go too, and she didn't look pleased. Maybe she had chores to do too. I hoped so.

A few others left, but new people were arriving all the time. Some of them brought food—sandwiches, fruit and fresh lemonade. Even a big box of donuts.

"I'm supporting this protest," said one woman. "I've got to go to work but I'll bring food and do anything else I can. My little girl was supposed to start kindergarten here."

After lunch I got bored. The bikers, except Duke, had gone into town. Grandma said that she wasn't sleeping in a tent with Mom, so she rode off with them. I heard her instructing Leon to drop her off at Aunt Gerry's so she could set up the guest room for herself. Peter left too. He said he needed to file his story and do some Internet research. He probably planned to do it from a comfortable motel room with high-speed Internet access, air-conditioning and a shower.

I wouldn't have minded a shower myself, but the closest one was locked up tight in the school gym. I stuck my head in the tent, thinking I'd take a nap, but it was hot and stuffy, so I grabbed my book and headed for the trees behind the playground. It was cooler in the shade. I found a comfortable place to sit, leaned back against a tree and started reading.

"Quite the kerfuffle," said a voice. I jumped and let out a yelp.

"Sorry. Didn't notice you were sleeping."

"I wasn't sleeping. What's a kerfuffle?" The gray-haired woman who

"Feud. I like that word. Yes, I'm feuding with Del. No sword fights, but I'm not going to speak to her ever again."

"I see."

We sat in silence for a while. Then Janie stood up and stretched. "Time to head back. It's hot and I wouldn't mind a shower."

"Me too," I said wistfully.

"Nice talking to you—what's your name anyway?"

"Callie."

"See you around, Callie." She put a leg in a stirrup and in one smooth movement was back on her horse.

After she left, I got up too. I couldn't have a shower, but maybe a nap would be the next best thing, even in a hot stuffy tent. It *had* been a sleepless noisy night. Mom was busy making protest signs to wave when the TV crews showed up, if they ever did. The tent was empty—and quiet.

I lay down on top of the sleeping bag but was still hot. I was too tired to care. Listening to the buzz of a yellow jacket, I fell asleep.

The drumming woke me. Drumming? I sat up and rubbed my eyes.

Mom yanked the tent flap aside. "Callie, wake up! A women's drumming circle is here. Come and listen! Oh, the music is amazing."

"What's a drumming circle?"

"They're supporting the protest," said Mom, ignoring my question. "Two of the women have children at Shady Glen School. I wish Gerry had told me there were First Nations people involved. I would have researched their culture."

Oh, no! Mom had said that word, *culture*.

I hate it when she goes into one of her "culture" stages. She spent a whole month the summer I was ten dragging me around art galleries—that was her modern art stage. Last winter had been her opera stage. She made me listen to hours of opera music and rented videos of operas. I didn't know they even made videos of operas! Some of the costumes were great and one video had lots of sword fights, but there was too much singing. Mom's opera phase had been pretty bad, but it hadn't lasted very long.

Well, if Mom was planning on learning about First Nations culture, I guess I could handle it. I liked the music.

"Isn't it wonderful?" said Mom. "One of the drummers is an elder!"

She was almost wriggling with excitement. "Come and listen to the chants. Hurry up!"

I brushed my fingers through my hair. My comb was still in my suitcase. I'd look for it later.

A crowd had gathered around the drummers. The five women were standing in the shade of the big tree by the cook shack. "How come it's called a drumming *circle* when they're standing in a straight line?" I asked.

"Just listen to the music," said Mom. She didn't have an answer to that one.

The drummer with the biggest drum had long gray braids that swung as she played. The others had smaller drums, and one woman was singing. Then the rest joined in and the music got louder.

"Hey! Those Indians make cool music!" Duke had joined us.

My mother gasped. "You shouldn't say 'Indians,' Duke. It isn't politically correct." She looked around as if she were afraid someone might have heard him.

"Huh? I don't do politics," said Duke.

"It's not politics, Duke. It's being polite," explained Mom. "Call them First Nations people or Aboriginals, okay?"

Then she looked doubtful. "At least I think those terms are right. These politically correct words change so fast that it's hard to keep up."

"Hey, I didn't mean to be rude," said Duke. "At least not with my words. But my body is going to be seriously rude if it doesn't get a shower soon."

"Didn't you stay in a motel last night? Didn't it have a shower?" I asked.

"Yeah, but this morning the other guys were still sleeping so I snuck out for breakfast."

"You had breakfast when you got here too," I pointed out.

"I was hungry. So what?"

"It's your belly. You can have all the breakfasts you can store in it. Why didn't you go into town with the other bikers?"

"I saw burgers on the grill for lunch." He sniffed his armpit. "Whew! Sure wish there was a shower around here."

"There's one in the school," I said. "I saw it when we went to Del's Christmas concert two years ago."

"There's a shower in the school?" said Duke. "What are we waiting for?"

"There's two, actually. One in the boys' changing room, one in the girls'. But we can't get into the school. It's locked."

"Locked? That's too bad," said Duke. "Maybe I'll go for a walk. Catch you later." He winked at me and sauntered off toward the school.

"I'll be back soon, Mom," I said. Duke was up to something, and I wanted to find out what it was.

Mom didn't respond. She was watching the drummers intently, her head moving to the music. She didn't notice me leave.

"Wait for me, Duke," I called. We walked slowly around the school, Duke eyeing every door. There was a covered play area on one side of the school, sort of a big open basement. A place for the kids to hang out when it was raining. Or when it was snowing. It snowed here in the winter. Snowed a lot.

Hopscotch squares were painted on the cement floor. Duke hopped and skipped along them, his gut jiggling each time his feet hit the ground. Then he walked very casually over to a door in the far corner.

"Keep an eye out," he said. Pulling something from his pocket, he bent over the lock. There was a grunt (from Duke) and a click (from the door). "No alarm," he said. "They really should install an alarm. This isn't even a dead-bolt lock." He shook his head as he swung the door open. "You'd think they'd know better."

He grinned at me and slipped through the door. "See you later, Little Lady."

"Duke, you can't…"

"Hey, I ain't going to steal nothing. I just want a shower, that's all. Nothing illegal about wanting to get clean."

The door closed behind him. I hoped he'd leave it unlocked when he came out. As soon as I found my suitcase and dug out shampoo and a towel, I was going to check out the shower in the girls' change room.

As Duke said, there was nothing illegal about wanting to be clean. Was there?

Chapter Seven

"It's the cops! Get out of there!" Duke's voice echoed down the empty hallway. Even with the shower going I heard him.

Maybe showering *was* illegal in the country. Del always smelled as if she thought it might be.

Duke had agreed to be my lookout while I showered. The last time I had seen him he was playing hopscotch again, using his bike keys as a marker and scattering drops of water from his wet hair on every square. He wasn't wearing his T-shirt, just his vest. I guessed he'd used the T-shirt as a towel. But now he was yelling at me. "Hurry up, Little Lady."

The siren had stopped wailing by the time I slipped out the door. Duke said, "Your hair's wet. How you going to explain that?"

"Maybe no one will notice. How are you going to explain *your* wet hair?"

He looked indignant. "I don't do explaining," he said. "It's like politics."

No one noticed that either of us had wet hair. There were more interesting things going on.

In front of the main door of the school there was a standoff between about a hundred people and two police officers. Bouncing around the edges of the crowd, trying to get pictures or sound bites, were the reporters who had finally arrived.

Even CBC was here—I saw their logo on one of the vans in the parking lot. There were reporters with cameras, reporters with video cams and reporters with microphones.

I edged behind Duke and tried to be invisible. He was certainly big enough to hide me. I hoped the reporters wouldn't recognize Mom. Or me. Mom would be happy to be the center of media attention again. Only this time she didn't have to chain herself to a tree to do it.

But the reporters weren't interested in either me or Mom. They had spotted Del and Radish at the edge of the playground. Within seconds the reporters surrounded the two of them, forgetting about the protesters in front of the school. I hoped they watched where they walked. Radish had been busy decorating the grass.

Duke and I followed the reporters, stepping carefully. Del frowned when she saw everyone coming toward her. Then the reporters began with their questions.

"Are you are a student here?"

"What grade are you in?"

"Do you ride your horse to school?"

"What's its name?"

"Can you take the horse close to the school so we can get a picture?"

"How do you feel about the school being sold?"

Del frowned again. "Go away," she said.

The reporters didn't go away, they moved closer. Radish looked even more unhappy than Del, and he gave that snickering sound again. This time it didn't sound like a laugh—it sounded like he was angry.

The reporters asked more questions.

"What are you and the other students doing to prevent the school closing?"

"How about we get the drummers to pose with you and the horse?"

"Riding a horse to school! It's history coming alive."

"I don't ride my horse to school," shouted Del. "I take the school bus. Like a normal kid."

Radish snorted, and then both of them were gone, galloping across the playground toward the woods. So, Del didn't like being interviewed any more than I did. I almost yelled, "Go for it, cuz." But I still wasn't speaking to her.

"Wow, that kid can ride as fast the Lone Ranger himself. Look at her go!"

The reporters headed back to the school. I heard one of them swear as she picked up a stick and scraped at her shoe.

The police were still standing on the lawn in front of the school, arms crossed. Some of the parents had moved up the school steps. I cringed when I saw

Mom in the front row. She was waving a sign that said *Save Shady Glen School!* A woman beside her ducked as Mom's sign narrowly missed her head. "Police brutality," yelled Mom. "Threatening women and children. This is shameful behavior. Shameful!"

One of the policemen stepped forward. He looked confused. "Excuse me, ma'am," he said, "there's been no brutality. We're here at the request of the school board. They want to make sure their property is protected."

"*Their* property, Constable?" someone yelled loudly. "This is community property! The school belongs to all of us."

Aunt Gerry was back. She pushed through the crowd to stand beside Mom. She carried a sign that said *Don't sell our school!*

"Shame on you," she shouted at one of the policemen. "Your mother went to this school. Why aren't you protesting with us?"

He took a step backward. "Excuse me, ma'am, but where my mom went to school isn't any of your business. I've got to do my job."

A man holding a sign that read *Education is priceless; schools are worth any price* said, "Our kids need this school. It's a crime to close it. You should arrest the school board members, officers."

"They've got no right to sell our school," someone else said.

"Look," said the young policeman, "I'm just doing what I'm told. If you've got complaints, don't tell me. Talk to..."

"Talk to me," said a new voice. "I'm Denis Ratchet, the chairman of the school board. Put down those ridiculous signs. I'm here to discuss your concerns."

It grew quiet. "Maybe you should have discussed things with us before now," said my aunt. Her voice sounded even louder than usual in the quiet.

"We did! We met with the parents of Shady Glen School in May." He pointed at the crowd. "Most of you were at that meeting. You knew that something had to be done."

"Something?" yelled my aunt. "You're doing *something* all right. The wrong thing."

"We had no choice. None!" said Mr. Ratchet. He was shouting almost as loudly as my aunt and his finger was waving wildly in the air, keeping time to his words. "We had no choice!"

"You didn't tell us you were going to sell our school," shouted Aunt Gerry.

The chairman lowered both his voice and his finger. "The repairs are too expensive. We had no choice but to sell. I regret that there wasn't time to arrange for community input, but the decision had to be made quickly."

My aunt interrupted him. "How about we do some inputting right now?"

Mr. Ratchet hesitated. "As long as you understand that…"

"Yeah, yeah," said Duke. "We get it. You had no choice. You told us that already. But you gotta talk to these nice people."

"Of course," said the chairman, smiling nervously at Duke.

I didn't like the chairman's smile. It showed too many of his teeth. "Put down those signs, and then we'll talk," he said. "Talk reasonably. We are all reasonable people, aren't we?" He smiled again.

No one answered, but all through the crowd signs were lowered. People began making their way to the picnic tables beside the cook tent.

The drums had been silent, but they began again, and the women started singing a new song. I hoped it was a song of peace.

Chapter Eight

"Coffee's on," said my aunt. "Help yourselves." There was cold pop as well. I grabbed a can. Other people got mugs of coffee or herbal tea. The chairs were still set up from the morning meeting. Once those were full, people sat on the grass.

When everyone had settled down, Mr. Ratchet went to the front of the group. He smiled and his teeth gleamed. "I apologize for the lack of communication," he began. "I was away—it *is* August after all. Even school board members deserve a holiday. This offer from B.J. Hyde was made just a few weeks ago. By the time I could convene a board meeting to discuss the situation, the deadline was upon us and…"

"What deadline?" asked my aunt.

"B.J. Hyde offered to purchase the school and the property around it. At a very generous price, I might add. But we only have a few days to agree to the sale or the offer will be withdrawn."

"So you were going to sell our school without even telling us?" shouted my aunt. "That's not right. We voted for you, Denis Ratchet, because we thought you'd be fair and honest."

"Selling the school isn't dishonest," he replied. He was shaking his finger again. "We—the members of the school board—were elected to manage the affairs of this school district the best way we can. That includes making some very difficult decisions."

"Difficult? You bet it's difficult. And now that we know about your plan, it will be even more difficult." My aunt was angry. "You can't do this, Denis! We're going to keep our school open, no matter how long we have to camp here."

Cameras flashed, video cams whirled. I knew that I'd hear my aunt's words again on tonight's television news. Then I remembered that I didn't have a TV, or even a radio.

Mr. Ratchet wasn't smiling anymore. "Listen, Gerry," he said. "Everyone, be reasonable. We have no choice. What else can we do? The school is nearly fifty years old and..."

"It's one of the oldest schools in the whole district," said a man. "I was once a student here myself. In the same class as the constable's mother, actually."

The policeman stared straight ahead, pretending he hadn't heard.

"People, you have to be realistic," Mr. Ratchet said. "Enrollment is down. The cost of the repairs is enormous…"

"Our taxes are enormous too," said my uncle.

"The bottom line is that the school board doesn't have the money to repair the school. This offer to purchase came at an opportune time."

"Why would anyone want to buy a school?" asked the man who had been a student here. "What good's a school to anyone but kids and teachers?"

Mr. Ratchet looked surprised. "I thought you all would have heard by now. This community is full of gossip… er, I mean people who know everything that goes on."

"Up till a few days ago, no one had any idea that our school was going to be closed, much less sold!" My aunt's face was bright red. She was *very* angry now.

"Well, I *am* surprised," said Mr. Ratchet. "I was sure you were all conversant with the details by now."

Duke stood up. "Enough," he shouted. "Talk so we can all understand. How come you agreed to sell this school and didn't bother telling anyone? Don't sound fair to me."

I tugged at his arm. "The policemen are looking at you," I whispered.

Duke sat down quickly.

"I don't see how this issue concerns you." Mr. Ratchet pointed at Duke. "Or the others here. You're not residents of this community. Who are you people? How is this your business?"

Unfortunately, my mom decided that she had been quiet for long enough. "We care about every child's right to receive an education. That's our business." She stood up and began waving her sign again. "Save the school," she yelled. "Save the school."

Other people joined in. Signs popped up all through the crowd like umbrellas in a rainstorm.

"Save the school!" The big drum picked up the rhythm, and the smaller drums began. People who didn't have signs to wave began to clap in time to the drumbeats.

The chanting got louder. The drumming got louder. Mr. Ratchet had his mouth open wide, showing lots of teeth. You couldn't hear what he was saying, but it was probably "we had no choice."

No one heard the motorbikes. They came roaring up the side of the driveway marked *Exit Only, Do Not Enter*.

My grandmother was once again perched on the back of Leon's bike.

Gran's red helmet shone as if she had just polished it. So did the purple, green and orange helmets worn by three other passengers on the backs of three other motorbikes.

Leon propped his bike up on its kickstand and helped Gran down. She whipped off her helmet and pulled out a big hat covered with red roses from the large bag she was carrying. She plunked the hat on her head.

The purple, green and orange helmeted figures climbed down from the bikes. Three hats covered with flowers replaced the colored helmets.

The Singing Grannies had arrived.

Chapter Nine

This would be an excellent time for me to leave, I decided. Grandma still hadn't managed to give me that hug. I took a casual step backward.

"There you are, Callie. Come here, please. We've made copies of our protest song so everyone can join in. I need you to pass them out." She handed me a stack of paper, luckily forgetting about the hug. "Make sure everyone gets one."

"Who *are* you people?" shouted Mr. Ratchet. "What are you doing here? This is private property. We will not allow a biker gang and their...uh... their...groupies to..."

"Please do not refer to us as a gang," said Leon. "We are just people who like to ride. We're a club, not a gang. You've been watching too much TV."

"Nor are these ladies and I 'groupies,' young man," said my grandmother. "These are some of the famous Singing Grannies. They've come to protest the closing of my granddaughter's school."

"Your *granddaughter*?" said Mr. Ratchet. He looked at my aunt. "I am not usually a betting man, Gerry, but I would wager a hundred dollars that this woman is your mother." He shook his finger at my aunt and then at my grandmother.

Mom waved her sign. "She's Rose Powers and she's also *my* mother," she said. "I'm Dian. My daughter is here too. Or she was. Where *is* Callie anyway?"

I had finished handing out the papers, and was standing beside the cook tent. I ducked inside. This was one introduction I wanted to avoid.

Cheers and applause erupted in the crowd. "It's a sister act," said someone, laughing. "Way to go, Gerry!"

"Just call us the Flower Power bunch," said my grandmother. "Bunch. Flowers. Get it?"

There was a groan. "That's wicked, Rose," said Leon. "But don't forget us."

My grandmother held up her hand. "Quiet please, everyone. Allow me to introduce Leon and his friends. Most of the Singing Grannies couldn't come on this trip, so these gentlemen agreed to join our group. Temporarily."

"We call ourselves the Belly Tones," said Leon. "The Singing Grandpas doesn't have the same ring to it as…"

Duke interrupted. "I picked the name," he announced. "Cute, hey?" He got up and headed over to join the other singers.

The bikers pulled off their helmets. They took wraparound sunglasses from their pockets, put them on and then moved to stand behind the Singing Grannies.

"Ready?" said a grannie wearing a hat decorated with orange flowers. She stepped in front of the group and waved her hands around like a conductor. "Lots of volume, girls. Oh, sorry. Girls and… guys. One, two, three…"

To the tune of "This Land is Your Land" the grannies and the bikers sang, "This school's a good school, a very fine school. Please keep it open, don't shut it down."

"Sing along everyone," said my grandmother. Everyone did. Everyone except Mr. Denis Ratchet and the policemen.

And me.

Chapter Ten

I wanted to get far away from my grandma (with her biker boyfriend) and my mom (with her protest sign) and my aunt (who was singing loudly and off-key). This was too much family. Way too much family. Very embarrassing family. I'd rather hang out with Duke, but he was doing his best to embarrass me too.

Staying out of sight as much as I could, I made my way to the covered play area. No one noticed me. They were too busy singing and waving protest signs. Everyone sang the chorus the loudest. "This school's a good school, a very fine school. Please keep it open, don't shut it down" was very clear. But you couldn't understand the other verses, except for a few words like "education" and "freedom" and "children's rights."

I was hoping that the school door was still unlocked and I could hide in the school. If the library had a computer I could message my friends in Vancouver. They would be wondering where I was. Mom had rushed me away so quickly that I hadn't even had time to check my e-mail.

Maybe I could stay in the school until the protest was over. On second thought, maybe I'd come out for meals and sneak back in. But there was no way I was going to sing. Or wave a sign. Or let anyone take my picture and put it on TV like the last time. Or let the reporters interview me and discover my full name! I had my hand on the doorknob when someone said, "You're not allowed to go in the school."

Del was sitting in the shadows.

Yanking my hand back, I said, "I'm not going anywhere." Then I remembered that I wasn't speaking to my cousin, so I started to walk away.

"I saw," said Del.

I was going to have to talk to her whether or not I wanted to. "Saw what?" I asked innocently.

"First that biker and then you. Going into the school."

"So?" I said.

"It's breaking and entering. You could go to jail."

"We didn't steal anything."

"It's still against the law. I bet that biker's been in trouble before. He looks mean."

"Duke's okay."

She stared at me in disbelief. "Come on! He's got tattoos."

"So what? I'm getting a tattoo next summer. My dad said I could."

"Really? What does your mom say?"

"She doesn't know yet."

Then I changed the subject. "Don't tell anyone we went in, okay?" I thought about adding "please" but remembered we were feuding. I don't think you're allowed to say "please" when you're feuding with someone.

Del looked scornful. "Of course I won't tell. Besides, I went in myself to use the bathroom because I hate that outhouse. I don't tattle."

It was my turn to be surprised. "Thanks."

We stared at each other for a few minutes and then I said, "See you around."

"Callie?" she said hesitantly. "Would you...would you help me? With Radish?"

"*What*?"

"It wasn't his fault you fell. He didn't understand. He thought you wanted to gallop. It was your fault."

"The stupid horse threw me off his back. How could it be *my* fault?"

She didn't answer. "After you fell, Mom said Radish was too old to be trusted. So I have to get rid of him."

"How do you mean 'get rid of him'?"

"Sell him. We've been advertising for months, but no one will buy him. Everyone's heard how you nearly got a concussion riding him."

I didn't say anything. "Even the new dude ranch won't want him," she went on. "If they bought him, then I could ride him once in a while. But they won't take him, after what happened to you. Poor Radish."

"Hey! I'm the one who got hurt."

"You weren't hurt badly. Radish didn't mean it."

"So why hasn't he apologized? He's still laughing at me."

"He's trying to talk to you," said Del. "That's his way of apologizing."

"Like I believe that!"

"Everyone thinks he's mean, but he's not. I've been riding him since I was four."

"I'm sorry you have to get rid of him," I said. "What's a dude ranch anyway?"

"It's like a camp, with horses and trail rides. Where city folks go to pretend to be cowboys."

"Not my idea of fun," I said, shuddering. "Besides, there isn't a dude ranch around here, is there?"

"There will be. That's why the school board is selling the school.

Mom found out that it's going to be turned into a touristy dude ranch."

I laughed. "Okay, so when the city cowboys aren't falling off horses, they'll go to school and learn how to speak horse language? What good is a school at a dude ranch?"

"Mom says it's the land that's valuable, said Del. "B.J. Hyde also bought the property behind the school. There's no way to get from that property to the highway except through the school grounds."

I thought about the wraparound driveway. "So the school will become a barn with a nice driveway? But if all of you local people are angry because the school is gone, then no one is going to visit the dude ranch, right? It will go broke."

Del shook her head. "Locals don't go to places like that," she said scornfully. "We have our own horses."

"So you and Radish won't ask for a job leading trail rides?" I asked. "Or cleaning out the stables? Or..."

"Not for a million dollars. I can't be a trail guide. I won't have a horse."

Even though I was still angry I felt sad for her. "Hey, Del, I'm sorry about Radish. I'd help if I could." Those were empty words. I knew there was nothing I *could* do. I patted her on the shoulder.

Then I yanked my hand away. I was *touching* my cousin. What next, a big family hug? Yuck.

I thought Del should be celebrating, not crying. No more school. No more demon horse. I patted her shoulder again.

It wasn't much, but it was the best I could do. I wasn't big on comforting. Besides, I was feuding with Del. Why did I care that she felt miserable?

Chapter Eleven

"Callie? Where are you? *Callie*!" Mom's voice was almost as loud as Aunt Gerry's. I thought about hiding, but I wasn't fast enough. My mother's head popped around the corner.

"There you are. The reporters want to do a family interview. They recognized me from the tree protest."

"I won't…"

"Don't you dare say 'won't' to me, Calendula Powers!" Mom's voice had that 'or else' tone.

"Bye, Del," I said, sighing. I sighed again when I saw the crowd of reporters in front of the school. They had surrounded my grandmother. I didn't actually see her, but there was a long-stemmed red rose bobbing above the reporters' heads. Gran and her hat had to be under that rose.

Mom pushed me into the crowd. "Hi again, everyone," she said. "This is my daughter, Calend…"

"Callie!" I shouted. "Just Callie."

"Her given name is Calend…"

"Mom!"

My mother looked hurt. "I don't know why you don't like your name. Your father chose it for you. I wanted to name you Daffodil, but…"

"Why would anyone in their right mind name a kid Daffodil?" asked a reporter.

"It's about that 'in their right mind' part," a photographer replied. "The whole family is named after flowers. Now, that's crazy to begin with."

"It isn't crazy at all, young man!" My grandmother was getting older, but there was nothing wrong with her hearing. "It's family tradition. My daughters, Dianthus and Geranium, have continued the tradition by naming their daughters Delphinium and…"

"Callie! Just Callie. Check out my cousin's horse if you want a weird name," I said to the reporters. "His name is Radish."

"Really? A horse Radish? I think I've met him—on a roast beef sandwich," someone said.

"We also have a goat named Turnip, a dog called Cabbage and Tomato the cat. There are too many flower names in my family, so I named our animals after vegetables," explained my aunt.

The photographer rolled his eyes and said quietly, "See? What did I say about 'in their right minds'?" After the laughter died down, the reporters went back to questioning Mom, Grandma and Aunt Gerry. No one was paying any attention to me, so I took a step backward. Time to make my escape.

"Don't go, Callie. Please tell them," said Del.

"Tell them what?"

"That Radish didn't mean to hurt you."

"Not a chance! Not a…"

"Please, Callie. Explain that he didn't understand what you wanted him to do."

"Why should I?" I asked in astonishment.

"Because if everyone knows it was a misunderstanding and it's in the paper and on TV, then maybe my parents will change their minds. Maybe they won't make me get rid of him."

"What are you two talking about?" asked my mother. She looked annoyed, but Grandma beamed. "This is Delphinium, my other granddaughter," she announced proudly. "She rides horses."

"We've already met your granddaughter and her horse," said the lady reporter that I had seen scraping at the bottom of her shoe. "I'm not doing a story about a horse. Particularly *that* horse." She turned back to Mom. "As I understand it, your first organized protest was a great success, Dian. Do you believe that...?"

"Please, listen to us!" said Del. "We want to explain about Radish. He's not a mean horse. Tell them, Callie."

The reporters looked confused, so Aunt Gerry explained. "Radish threw Callie last year. She had to go to the hospital. We didn't want anyone else getting hurt riding him, so we're getting rid of him."

"It's not fair, Mom," said Del. "He was just having a bad day."

"The *horse* had a bad day?" I said. "What about *my* bad day?"

"No one is making you leave your family because you made one mistake," Del said. "You get to stay with the people who love you. Radish doesn't."

"It's sad, but it isn't much of a story," said the lady reporter. "'Girl apologizes for horse. Horse says nothing.' Now, if Radish could tell us why he tossed Callie, that would be a great story."

Del glared at me. "It's your fault, Callie. Radish thought you wanted to gallop."

I glared back, sorry that I had wasted two perfectly good comforting pats on my cousin. "He should have known I didn't want to go faster."

"How could he know? You gave him the wrong signal. He's a horse, not a mind reader."

Some of the reporters were looking interested now. A photographer lifted his camera and pointed it in our direction. I didn't want this conversation repeated on the evening news, so I took Del's arm and began pulling her away.

"Let's talk somewhere else," I said.

"It was your fault, Callie. It *was*," Del said, but she let me lead her toward the playground. The reporters went back to asking Mom about her tree protest.

I sighed. Deeply. "Okay," I said. "You're right, it was my fault." At this point I'd say anything to shut Del up. "I apologize. I'm sorry. Now leave me alone."

My dad often says, "Talk is cheap." Well, saying I was sorry about Radish only cost me about half a cent.

"You *aren't* sorry," Del said. "If you really were, then you'd help." We were halfway across the playground by now and still reporter-free.

"I can't help. There's nothing I can do. I said I was sorry. Isn't that enough?"

"No."

"*No*? What do you mean, *no*?"

"You can fix things, Callie. All you have to do is ride Radish again."

I stared at her. "Why would I do that?"

Del sighed. "I knew it. You're scared."

"I'm not scared," I said. "I ended up in hospital the last time. Why should I do it again? I'd probably end up dead."

"You'll be fine as long as you don't kick him like you did last summer. That's why he took off."

"I lost my balance and grabbed him with my knees. My feet sort of banged against him accidentally. I wasn't kicking him on purpose, I was just trying to hang on."

"Please, Callie?"

"No, no, no! I'm sorry that you have to sell him, but…"

"You're chicken." She made a clucking sound. "Chicken. Sissy city girl, afraid of a horse. You're too scared to even try."

"Am not!"

Del clucked louder. "Hey, reporters, come here and see the chicken. Biggest chicken around. Big red-haired chicken with scrawny legs."

"Looked at your own legs lately?" I asked. I wanted to hit her, but I restrained myself and began to walk away instead.

"Chicken!" she yelled and clucked again.

"I am *not*! If Radish were here, I'd show you all that I'm not afraid. I'd ride him." The moment those words left my mouth I knew I'd regret them. And I did.

Del grinned. "Okay, do it. I dare you." She pointed behind me. Slowly, not wanting to see what she was pointing at, I turned around. Beyond the playground, almost hidden in the shade of a big cottonwood tree, was Radish.

He lifted his head and looked straight at me. He snickered. I heard him clearly. He was laughing.

Chapter Twelve

As slowly as I could, I followed my cousin. "Hey, Radish, look who's come to see you," she said, patting him. "It's Callie. Remember her?"

Radish snorted. He remembered.

"Uh, Del," I began, but she clucked again and I shut up. A dare was a dare.

She untied Radish and knotted his

reins together. "It's easier with the reins tied," she said. "Up you go."

I put one foot in a stirrup and pulled myself up. Radish snorted again. "I'm not sure," I began.

But Del wasn't listening. She was talking to Radish. "I know, I know. You don't want her to ride you. But this time it will be different. I'll tell her what to do. It will be all right." She patted him, and then she adjusted the height of the stirrups and handed the reins to me.

"Listen carefully. Here's what you do. Pull back on the reins slowly when you want him to stop. Don't yank them. Press your knees gently into his sides if you want him to go faster. And try not to let him know you're afraid."

"I'm *not* afraid," I said, but my voice was shaking. I tried to smile bravely but my smile was as shaky as my voice, so I turned it off.

"Are you ready?"

I wasn't ready. Not at all. But I had to go through with this.

I swallowed hard and nodded. Slowly, easily, gently, Radish and I began moving. Out of the trees, across the playground.

Del walked beside us. I let myself breathe. So far, so good, I thought. When Radish moved, I could feel myself move with the same rhythm. Slowly, gently, easily.

Past the swings. Past the campfire. I sat straighter. Tried a smile. It stayed on my face.

"You're doing great," Del said.

"Thanks," I said.

"Oh, I was talking to Radish. But you're doing fine too, Callie."

"We can go faster," I said. "I've got this riding thing figured out."

"Okay, press your knees gently into his sides and make sure you aren't pulling back on the reins. Do it slowly."

Slowly I pressed my knees into Radish. He began to move faster. Not much faster, just enough. My smile got bigger.

"Don't let him go near the highway," called Del. She had stopped trying to keep up with us. "As soon as the reporters see you, pull back on the reins, and he'll stop. Then you can explain how gentle he is and…"

"No problem," I called back. "Don't worry. Everything's under control."

It was. I was riding a horse and I wasn't scared. I *did* have it all under control.

Radish's ears twitched backward. "You're okay, horse," I said. "We're both okay."

A couple of little kids watched us go by. I lifted one hand and waved at them. They waved back. This was almost fun.

Radish and I moved past the cook tent and around the corner of the school. The reporters were still clumped around my family. Some of the Grannies and the Belly Tones were sitting on the grass, studying the words to the protest song. I heard Duke say, "How about we make up another song? With easier words?" The chairman of the school board had found a seat. He looked hot and was wiping at his forehead with a handkerchief.

The drummers were on the school stairs, singing softly, as if they were practicing. Like everyone else, they didn't notice Radish and me.

But when the woman with the biggest drum suddenly banged it loudly, Radish noticed the drummers.

He reared up on his hind legs. I dropped the reins and grabbed the saddle horn, trying to stay on his back. Radish whinnied and his front legs came down with a thump. Then he bolted.

Suddenly everyone noticed us.

"Quick, get a shot of that," shouted a reporter. "Wow! Hope the kid can stay on until we get a picture."

"Hey, Little Lady, be careful."

"Callie, stop," called my mother. "Get off that horse immediately."

For once I really wanted to obey my mother, but Radish was moving too quickly for me to do anything but hang on as if my life depended on it. Maybe it did. My feet flew out of the stirrups and banged against Radish's sides. He went faster. I shut my eyes and lowered my head as far as I could. The light flickered through my closed eyelids—now we must be in the woods behind the school. I hoped Radish wouldn't run under a low tree branch and knock me off.

It felt as if I'd been clinging to Radish for hours, but it couldn't have been that long. Thankfully, he hadn't reared up again. What was I going to do? Would he stop running when he was tired? How long would that take?

His feet made a thundering noise. I squeezed my eyes shut and held on. I should have been praying, but all I could think was, If I live through this, I'll make Mom take me home. Today.

Radish ran. I hung on. The sun seemed brighter. Maybe we had left the trees behind.

His thundering hooves thundered louder. It sounded like two horses were racing, side-by-side. Then a voice said, "Whoa, slow down, boy. Easy does it."

Radish whinnied and jerked his head back. Miraculously, he slowed. Then stopped. I slowly opened my eyes.

Chapter Thirteen

Another horse *was* beside us. "Are you all right, Callie?" asked Janie. "Easy does it, Radish." She leaned across her own horse's neck and patted Radish. "Easy, easy. Good boy."

Her gray hair was standing up around her head—she must have lost her cowboy hat as she chased after us. She held Radish's reins in one hand.

"You're a great runner, Radish," she said. "Took me a while to catch up. Are you all right, Callie?"

My mouth was open to say, "I'm fine, thank you," but instead I burst into tears. "I messed up. I messed up again," I sobbed.

"No, you didn't. It wasn't your fault he bolted. When that drum started up so close to him, he got scared."

"So did I!"

She smiled at me. "You did well. You stayed on. Lots of people, even some experienced riders, would have fallen off."

I unclenched one hand from the saddle horn and rubbed at my eyes. "Really? I did okay?"

"Just fine. You could be a good rider, with a bit of practice. But right now why don't you take a break? Sit for a while. When you're rested, we'll head back. The others will be worried about you."

The others! Del. Mom. The reporters would have their story after all: *Girl on runaway horse rescued. Girl okay. Horse in big trouble.*

I fought back tears again. "Del will lose Radish. It's my fault. Again."

Janie got down from her horse, and then she helped me dismount.

"Does he ground tie?" she asked and then shook her head. "You probably don't know. Let's try it." She dropped both sets of reins to the ground. Both horses stood still. "Yup. He's well trained," she said, pulling a water bottle from her saddle pack. "He'll stay right here while you rest."

My legs felt as if they were made of play dough. I sat down, hard, on the ground and took a gulp of the water Janie handed me. "Thanks."

"You're shaken up. Take deep breaths. It will turn out all right."

I took another gulp of water. "It won't be all right. Radish is in worse trouble now—he ran away with me. Del will have to get rid of him for sure."

"Maybe not. He didn't throw you, did he?"

"Not this time."

"What made you ride him again?"

"Del dared me."

She nodded. "Well, you certainly put a stop to the kerfuffle about the school being sold. Everyone was running after you until I told them to stay put or they'd scare Radish and he'd never stop."

"But the school is still going to be closed, and Del will still lose Radish. I didn't help at all."

"You can't do anything about the school. Forget it."

"It's not fair. Just because some rich person wants…"

"Hold on. There will be lots of jobs on the dude ranch—groomers, trainers, trail guides. There's also going to be a restaurant that sells local beef. It will need dishwashers, waiters, lots of help. Turning the school into a dude ranch will be good for Shady Glen."

"It won't. The local people won't work there. Del said she wouldn't work at the dude ranch for a million dollars."

I poured some water on my hands and rubbed them across my face, getting rid of any tear tracks. I was going to ride Radish back to the school, sitting tall in the saddle, smiling. I was going to pretend that I'd meant for him to gallop away.

Probably no one would believe me, but it was worth a try. Maybe Aunt Gerry would let Del keep her horse when she saw that I was still riding him.

Janie frowned. "Hadn't realized people would miss this old school so much that they'd turn down good jobs," she said. "That's plain silly."

"*Everyone* will miss the school," I said. "I'm not going to wave a sign or sing a protest song, but the protestors are right. It's wrong for the school board to do this."

"But if they can't afford to keep the school open, what…?"

I took a deep breath before I spoke. "I know how they could keep the school and sell it at the same time."

She stared at me. "What are you talking about?"

I sighed and said, "Forget it. It was just an idea I had this morning. It probably wouldn't work anyway."

Janie held out her hand to me to help me up. "So, before we head back, you want to share your idea with me?"

My legs no longer felt like play dough when I stood up. "Why do you want to know?" I asked. "You don't live here. Why do you care?"

She didn't look at me as she picked up her horse's reins. "I'm curious."

Radish whimpered as I approached him. "It's me again," I said. "Sorry, but we've got to ride back. Don't you realize I'm trying to help you? Just behave and maybe you won't have to leave Del."

He lowered his head and nudged my sleeve.

"You and that horse are going to get on fine," Janie said. "He likes you."

"Really? He *likes* me?"

She boosted me onto Radish's back and checked the stirrups. "So, you going to tell me your idea?"

I shrugged. "If you want. This B.J. Hyde is rich, right? Really rich?"

Janie nodded. "That's what people say."

"Okay, then why doesn't he repair the school, keep it open and let everyone keep on using it?"

"But what about the dude ranch?"

"It can still be built. There's lots of room for the stables and restaurant and everything else a dude ranch needs and for the school too."

She laughed. "Sounds like a good deal for the school board and the people of Shady Glen. But what does B.J. Hyde get out of it? Besides spending a truckload of money?"

"Publicity. Lots of publicity. All the TV stations, radio stations and newspapers would report how the school was saved. Everyone would know about the new dude ranch even before it's built. People would want to come stay here because the owner is such a...a...what's that word that means someone who gives other people lots of money?"

"Philanthropist," she said. I looked at her blankly, so she explained, "Like a sponsor. Or a patron."

"Right. Philan...sponsor. B.J. Hyde could sponsor the school."

She thought for a moment. "A story like that would be excellent publicity for a new dude ranch," she said.

"There's plenty of competition for tourist dollars these days."

"Not from me!" I said. "Paying money to ride a horse isn't my idea of a fun holiday."

She grinned. "You might change your mind. You ready to go back?"

"Let's show them we can do this," I said to Radish, patting his neck. I picked up his reins and nudged him gently. We moved off slowly.

Janie swung herself up onto her horse. "Actually, the school's back the other way," she said, coming up beside us. "Mind if I ride with you?"

"Um. Sure. That would be okay," I said. I looked around. We were in the middle of a huge open field. I could see trees in the distance. We had come a long way from the school. Radish followed Janie's horse as she headed toward the trees. We rode in silence for a while. I could smell the grass and feel the wind tickling the back of my neck.

"This isn't so bad."

"Told you so," said Janie. "You know, that's an interesting idea of yours."

"I get good ideas all the time. Usually no one listens to me." I sighed as loudly as my Aunt Gerry. "After all, I'm just a kid."

"Hadn't noticed," she said. "Want to canter?"

Cantering, it turned out, was much like galloping—only smoother. It was faster than I would dare ride if I were alone. When I could see the school ahead of us, I was almost disappointed.

"Okay, Radish," I said to him. "Let's show them."

As if I'd been on a horse all my life—at least I hope that's what I looked like—Radish and I cantered through the playground toward the school.

"So I see," said Peter. "Listen everyone. I've found out something really interesting. The person who…"

No one was listening. "Move back, everyone. You're making Radish nervous," said Del. "Give him some room."

I reached down and patted his neck. "It's okay. You're doing fine."

"You're both doing great," said Del, trying not to sound surprised. "I can't believe you're still on his back! When he bolted, I thought you'd be flat on the ground in no time."

"She handled him well," said Janie. "This girl's got the makings of a good rider."

"I need to tell you what I found out," Peter said loudly. "It's important."

"Whatever it is, it will keep, Peter," said my mother. "No one is interested right now."

Duke lifted me off Radish's back. "That horse took off so fast I figured you wouldn't be back until midnight. The guys were going to ride out and see if we could find you, but the horsey woman said she'd bring you back."

I shuddered, thinking of what Radish's reaction would be to a half dozen loud motorcycles roaring up behind him.

Mom threw her arms around me. "Oh, Callie. I was so worried." She turned her head so the reporters could get a better shot of her face. "My precious child is safe."

"Mom!" I pushed her away. "Mom, it wasn't a big deal. Stop hugging me."

Denis Ratchet joined us. "I'm sure this young lady will appreciate the new dude ranch. She can visit next summer and take riding lessons." He smiled at the cameras. "Why don't you tell the world about this little girl and her narrow escape? Next summer you can do a follow-up story when she learns to ride properly."

"Callie doesn't need lessons," shouted Aunt Gerry. "She just needs more practice. She can go riding with Del and Radish."

"Mom? Does that mean that I can keep him?" Del had her horse's reins in her hand. "Can he stay?"

My aunt nodded. "For now."

The reporters were smiling. "A happy ending! I love happy endings," one said. "Can we get a shot of both girls and the horse? Over by the school…"

The school. Suddenly it grew very quiet.

"Well, maybe not entirely a happy ending," said the reporter softly. "There's still the school problem."

Del and I walked Radish around to the front of the school. Everyone followed us. Still no one spoke. The drumming circle was silent. The Singing Grannies didn't even hum. No one shouted, "Save the school." The protest signs stayed facedown on the grass, and the chairman didn't tell us how he had no choice. Not even a robin chirped.

I tried to smile. "Well, we saved your horse, Del."

"But not the school," she said sadly.

"Excuse me, please. I'd like to say something." Janie got down from her horse, made her way to the front of the school and climbed the stairs. When she reached the top step she turned around and faced everyone. "There's something I need to tell you."

Oh, no! I thought. She's going to tell them she stopped Radish, that I couldn't do it. I hadn't exactly lied, but I hadn't explained that Janie had rescued me. Without her help, Radish—with me clinging to his back—would probably still be running.

Janie must have known what I was thinking because she smiled at me and shook her head slightly.

"Okay, here goes," she said. "My name is B.J. Hyde."

There was a loud gasp from the crowd. "You? I thought he was a him," I said.

"Nope. B.J. stands for Barbara Jane. But I usually go by Janie, except when I'm doing business."

"*That's* what I've been trying to tell you," said Peter. "I found her picture on the Internet."

"You've been spying," said my mother. "That's not fair. You should have told us who you were."

"I *was* going to tell you," Janie answered. "But then I saw which way the wind was blowing. With all those angry words I figured I'd keep quiet. Now, don't you start waving those signs or singing again. Hear me out."

"Talk fast, lady," said Duke. "Then leave. You ain't real popular around here."

"I know," she said. "But please, try to understand. When I offered to buy Shady Glen School, I knew nothing about it except that it needed repairs and didn't have many students. I didn't know how much it meant to the community. I've learned a lot."

"I don't care what you've learned," said Duke. "What are you going to *do* about it?"

"That's the hard part," she admitted. "I've already bought the land behind the school. I've paid the architect to design the bunkhouses and stables. I've even hired a chef for the restaurant. I've dreamed of owning my own dude ranch for years. But I don't want to take away your school either. I didn't know what to do until a clever young woman shared her idea with me."

"I bet you mean Callie," said Peter.

Peter, Mom, Grandma and Duke smiled proudly. "She's a smart one," said Duke.

"She gets her intelligence from my side of the family," said my mother.

"Mom!"

"I agree, she's smart," said Janie Hyde. "And I'm going to do what she suggested. I'm still going to buy the school. But I'll pay for the repairs, and when it's fixed up, I'll let you all use it. The kids can go to school, and you can still have square dances and 4-H meetings and all of that. But the school board has to pay the teachers and the janitor, agreed?"

"Agreed!" shouted Aunt Gerry.

"What do you think, Mr. Ratchet?"

"Uh…um…I have to consult the other members of the board. But I don't see why they won't agree."

"Good! Maybe we can talk about changing the school's name. After all, if I'm sponsoring it…"

"We need to talk to our lawyer too," said Mr. Ratchet. "He'll have to make up a new agreement. But he's away on holiday for a month, so we can't..."

"I'll help with that," said Leon. My grandmother smiled at him. "I'm half retired, but the other half of me is still a lawyer. I'll draw up your legal agreement. For free."

"I appreciate that," said Janie.

"Maybe we—the community—can help with the repairs," said my aunt. "We've got a gravel pit on our land— we'll donate the gravel for the new septic field."

"Hey, I can fix the wiring, so the kids can use computers in the classrooms," said Duke.

Everyone stared at him. "Don't look at me like that. Nothing wrong with having a job, is there?"

"You're an electrician?" said Peter. "Never would have guessed it."

"Don't have to work a lot," said Duke. "I own the company, so I take time off whenever I want. To go riding with the guys and stuff like that."

"You're a boss?" I stared at Duke in disbelief.

Leon laughed. "Hard to believe, isn't it? Beneath all those tattoos is a smart businessman."

Other people were shouting out offers of help. "I put a new roof on my barn last year," someone said. "There's enough material left over to fix the school roof. We'll have a work bee."

"And a huge garage sale. To buy new equipment for the gym."

"I know an office that's upgrading their equipment. I can get computers donated to the school," one of the Singing Grannies offered.

Everyone was smiling, even Mr. Ratchet. His smile didn't bother me anymore.

"This is wonderful. Thank you everyone," said Janie. "But I've got one condition you have to meet."

"Huh?" said Duke.

"One thing you have to agree to before we shake on this deal."

"Exactly what is this 'condition'?" asked Mr. Ratchet suspiciously.

"I want to use the school in the summer," she said.

"That sounds reasonable," said Mr. Ratchet. "I'm sure the other members of the school board will agree to that."

"Why do you want to use the school?" I asked.

"Got a bright idea of my own, Callie," she answered. "I'm going to open a summer school. For kids who need extra help with reading and arithmetic."

"Summer school?" I said. "No one wants to go to summer school."

"*Everyone* will want to come to my summer school," she said. "I'm going to hire me some top-notch teachers. The 'Three Rs Ranch and School,' that's what I'm going to name it."

"I've got it!" I said, laughing. "That's funny!"

She grinned. "Yup. This is going to be the only school in the world that teaches the 'real' Three Rs. The important things every kid needs to learn. Reading, Riding and 'Rithmetic."

Acknowledgments

The author would like to thank the B.C. Arts Council, Lillian Squalian and Maggie Ranger of the Nenqayni Drummers, Sheila Dick, Maureen Colgan, Heidi and Lexie Redl, Mrs. Hague's students at Murrayville Elementary School, The Wednesday Writers and Super-Editor Melanie Jeffs for their help, encouragement and support.

Ann Walsh loves horses as much her main character, Callie, does. Ann is the author of numerous books for children and young adults, including *Flower Power*, also in the Orca Currents series. Ann lives in Williams Lake, British Columbia.

orca currents

For more information on all the books
in the Orca Currents series, please visit
www.orcabook.com.